Layout design by Gary Lewis

Scripture taken from The Voice™. Copyright © 2012 by Ecclesia Bible Society. Used by permission. All rights reserved.

Lewis, Gary B, 1952-

An Epistle to an Apostle: Titus to Paul

ISBN: 978-0-6455552-8-8

1. Historical Fiction 2. Bible Study 3. Christian Discipleship

Printed in Australia

PUBLISHED BY GARY B LEWIS

Cranbourne East, VICTORIA 3977

gazzablew@bigpond.com

AN EPISTLE TO
AN APOSTLE

μια Επιστολή προς
έναν Απόστολο

Titus to Paul

από τον Τίτο στον Παύλο

Gary B Lewis

Hey Paul

I'm writing to you in desperation. Oh how I wish we could have lived in the twenty first century — so that we could have a zoom-chat, or I could at least send you an SMS. But here we are locked in the time warp of the first century A.D. ... How can I possibly begin sorting out anything in the midst of this cesspool of crudity, deceit and heresy on Crete?! It feels like I have been abandoned — leaving me so vulnerable. My stomach aches and my head hurts. Confusion and despair are my constant companions ...

'Hold the phone!'

Now that's a 20th century saying if ever there was one! I'm getting ahead of myself! I just realized ... we need to back up a bit and go through the proper protocols and introductions for the writing of a book! "Why?"

You may well ask. Hah! Actually, it's because you are reading this book in real time … sometime during the 21st century. So, I will do my best to abide by all the necessary formalities of publication. Starting with the Table of Contents, then the Preface, followed by the Introduction. Please hang in there whilst we plough through these formalities which will provide some background information. Hold the phone … and I'll get back to sharing my letter with you in a little while!

TABLE OF CONTENTS

PREFACE v

SECTION ONE:

- Introduction.......................................2
- Explanation.......................................6
- Titus writes to Paul — BEFORE 7

SECTION TWO:

- Interlude...29
- Paul writes to Titus........................33

SECTION THREE:

- Interlude...43
- Titus writes to Paul — AFTER 49
- Final Word.......................................77

APPENDIX:

- Discussion Questions 83
- End Notes / Bibliography...............87

PREFACE

The purpose of this book, '*An Epistle to an Apostle'*, is to explore the book in the Bible we call "Titus" — the epistle which Titus received from his mentor Paul. However, we will explore the epistle to Titus from a totally different perspective.

Underpinned by a deep respect for the scriptures, I will be exercising some degree of literary licence as I propose some thought-provoking questions from the young man, Titus. The intention for this writing, is to gain some suppositional insights into the life, mindset and circumstantial struggles of Paul's young protégé.

I hope and pray that the reader will engage in reading this book with grace — without prejudice or offence. I also pray that you may gather some helpful insights into the conjectural possibilities of Titus's thinking and the many questions raging through his head and heart.

Other helpful insights to be gained hopefully will be firstly who Titus was. What he was like as a Christian believer. What his concerns were. Where his missional work was to take place and what that work involved.

Whilst this book is not intended to be an in-depth study or theological presentation; it goes without saying, that in addition to extensively and respectfully reading through some Bible commentaries; this work has also required much historical and Biblical research and prayerful thought. In fact, the idea for this book was planted within my spirit almost 30 years ago, when I was studying at Bible College in Victoria, Australia. And over the years it has continued to take root within my head and spirit, and is now ready to spring forth.

In reading all of Paul's writings and his many encounters, you would be correct in forming the opinion that not only was he an exceptional apologetic of the Christian faith and scriptures; but he was also very formal in his approach to letter writing, viz., in the style of the day. He was very matter of fact and deeply serious in his manner. One could even go as far as to conclude that he never revealed any sense of light-heartedness at all.

The two main characters mentioned in the epistle to Titus, is the author — the Apostle Paul.

Then we have the recipient of the epistle — Titus. However, as the title of this conjectured book suggests, this is about Titus writing an epistle to his mentor, Paul.

In SECTION ONE, my intention is to be writing in the first person i.e. as Titus, in order to gain some speculative insights into the life, mindset and struggles of Paul's young protégé.

In the writing of this book, I have deliberately attempted to lighten things up a bit — albeit with a trace of prudish indifference and the slightest hint of larrikinism. The reader will be challenged to consider Titus's brashness, as well as his tirades of disconcerted questioning of the Apostle.

As I have already noted, Paul customarily used the formal protocols of his era to address his recipients. From my research, it seems that even the most contemporary paraphrased editions and translations, perpetuate this formality — especially his introductory paragraph. Hence, in SECTION TWO, I have deliberately chosen to use The Voice translation for its less formal approach.

Speaking of formats and styles of writing, before we begin to unpack this '*An Epistle to an Apostle*', let me explain something about the layout of this book. Following the Table of Contents and Preface, there will be the Introduction, where you'll be introduced to Titus himself, who will give you a brief overview of his life, calling and ministry.

The subsequent unfolding of this book will occur in three stages or sections.

However, before explaining the layout any further, let me suggest that if you have never read Paul's letter to Titus previously — then please

DO NOT READ IT NOW!!

The reason for this will become clear soon enough. However ... if the reader has previously read Paul's letter to Titus, and is familiar with its contents; then I strongly recommend that you try putting what you know to one side — at least in SECTION ONE, and allow '*An Epistle to an Apostle*', to speak for itself.

SECTION ONE

INTRODUCTION

Hello, my name is Titus.

I am Greek — a Gentile in other words. I'm not a Jew like Paul. My name looks the same in Greek as it does in Latin. However, in Latin is pronounced as *tee-tus,* whereas in Greek it is pronounced as *tee-tohs*. The name Titus is derived from the Greek word 'tio' meaning '*to honor*'.

You've probably heard of me as one of the protégés of the great apostle Paul. I became one of Paul's converts to the Christian faith when I was a young man and eventually joined him as a co-worker in the ministry.

Our first journey together took us all the way to Jerusalem (Galatians 2:1-3), because Paul was incensed about some Jewish brothers who had secretly spied on his work, and were pushing for the circumcision of Gentile converts. We set off so that Paul could put his case with the Church leaders against the circumcision of Gentile converts. Prior to this Paul has already had our colleague Timothy circumcised — due to the fact that he was half-Jewish.

Upon arriving in Jerusalem, we met with the apostles there and their leadership team. As I said, the topic was circumcision and whether or not Gentile converts should be circumcised. And due to the fact that I was a Greek Gentile (that's Greek with an 'r' if you please!), you could say that I became 'Exhibit-A'.

Paul's defence was basically that anyone could be a Christian without being circumcised, and that what mattered most was that God knows the heart of a person, and because of the completed work of Christ, He makes no distinction in giving the Holy Spirit to all who receive the gospel message. (Galatians 2:1-5; Acts 15: 1-30). "Neither circumcision nor uncircumcision means anything; what counts is a new creation." (Galatians 6:15) [1]

Fortunately, I came out of this whole encounter unscathed — praise God!

As one of Paul's associates, I also had the privilege of working alongside him on his third missionary journey to Ephesus. From there, Paul commissioned me to help with the work in the church at Corinth. (2 Corinthians 2:12-13; 7:5-6; 8:6)

Following Paul's release from his first stint in prison (Acts 28), we worked together on the island of Crete. After some time, Paul left me there as his representative to look after some things he was unable to complete. (Titus 1:5; 2:15; 3:12-13)

Later, it was pre-arranged that I would meet Paul at Nicopolis, on the west coast of Greece — once my replacement had arrived.

When I returned to Corinth, it was my honor and responsibility to deliver Paul's second letter to the church there. Whilst I was there, I also coordinated a 'go-fund-me' fundraising campaign for the needy families back in Jerusalem. (2 Corinthians 8:10, 17, 23)

My last recorded assignment under Paul's directive, was to leave on a missions trip to Dalmatia. (Encompassing the northern part of modern-day Albania, much of Croatia, Bosnia and Herzegovina, Montenegro, Kosovo and Serbia.)

And so, even before the wonders of technology and animation or film — yes I did see '101 Dalmatians'!

Historically, biblical scholars have accredited me as a rather capable and resourceful leader, considering my young age and the assignments given to me, by the great apostle himself. Therefore, it is only fitting for me to conclude this introduction, by quoting my mentor and friend: ' "Let him who boasts boast in the Lord." For it is not the one who commends himself who is approved, but the one whom the Lord commends.'

(2 Corinthians 10:17-18)[2]

EXPLANATION

The timeframe and structure for SECTION ONE is written intentionally to portray the backdrop of Titus's predicament *before* he received his letter from Paul.

This first section is designed to set the scene of Titus's desperate plight. It assumes that Titus has absolutely no idea of what he should be doing, as he depicts to Paul ... *off-loads* would be a better way to say it about the chaotic situation on Crete.

Now you are ready to read Titus's ***epistle to the Apostle*** as he attempts to reach out — to his spiritual father and mentor in the faith and ministry — for help.

TITUS WRITES
TO PAUL

BEFORE
HE RECEIVES
PAUL'S LETTER

Hey Paul

I'm writing to you in desperation. Oh how I wish we could have lived in the twenty first century — so that we could have a zoom-chat, or I could at least send you an SMS. But here we are, locked in the time warp of the first century A.D.

Now, I know that you are a true apostle of our Lord Jesus Christ. And I've heard you talk so much about truth, godliness and hope, but I'm really struggling to see the connection with these Christian principles amidst my current circumstances.

I feel swamped in a hotbox of untruths, deception and lies; and I just can't seem to find the balance between the common faith we share in God and the carnal worldliness of this place.

Paul, you know that I totally respect you as my father in the faith — right!? You introduced me to Jesus ... you discipled me ... you apparently recognized in me some leadership potential ... and now you've commissioned me as your understudy or stand-in here on Crete.

To say I'm drowning here is an understatement! I am so out of my depth, that it feels like the Mediterranean Sea has just swallowed the whole island in one giant tsunami of ungodliness. To be honest, I just don't know why you have left me here. Really Paul — to put it in plain language — I have no idea of what my job description is. I mean ... what do I do? ... where do I start? ... what can I do?

The situation here is so chaotic with too many wannabe bosses ravenous for position and power, but short on leadership. Many of the people have an insatiable hunger for money and loose living. Along with gossiping women — busybodies they are! Men and women getting drunk with little regard for truth or decency — with no thought of others — let alone the gospel of truth you introduced them to.

How can I possibly begin sorting anything out in the midst of this cesspool of crudity, deceit and heresy on Crete?! It feels like I have been abandoned — leaving me so vulnerable. My stomach aches and my head hurts. Confusion and despair are my constant companions.

It seems almost improbable that there is anyone who is above suspicion in any way. I mean, especially

in the Christian community you established, they are
no different from the wider community — or so it
appears. It's difficult to find anyone who shows any
sign of wholesomeness or integrity. They are such a
concoction of angry, dodgy, drunkards, pompous,
self-seeking nincompoops. Cretans — that's what
they are — through and through!

As a largely patriarchal society, the older men
in particular are the figureheads of anger,
deceptiveness and greed. They continually make up
stories of heroism and sweet dealings. Many of them
are either polygamists or womanizers — and they
boast about their exploits!

With my head-spinning observations, I have
been able to discern — both in their homes as well as
in the streets — that their children appear to be going

down a similar spiralling path of disruptive, deceptive and disrespectful behaviour.

Paul, there appears to be so many contradictions — no matter where I go. What I mean is that on one hand they display such fervour for their newfound faith after embracing your passionate preaching of the good news. And then on the other hand, they engage in such raucous living and fraudulent business dealings.

In my endeavours to be incarnational whilst intentionally staying connected with the Father — living with purpose — dwelling among the people and engaging authentically with others; I am finding in my conversations with a variety of people and across the age spectrum, that my senses are overwhelmed by their glazed looks, the reeking of alcohol, disrespect and crudeness of their innuendos.

Please forgive me Paul for ranting, but it's just that you haven't lived here as long as I have been here now. And whilst I was raised a 'good' Greek lad in a pagan society worshipping Greek gods along with all their unholy practices, including the carousing and revelry of Greek culture; what I am witnessing and experiencing here on Crete even makes **me** blush! What I am seeing and hearing is not only lamentable and embarrassing — it is ungodly.

Need I continue … ? Yes, I must — at the risk of sounding like a broken record (although they haven't been invented yet!) I desperately need you to understand how I am feeling, right at this moment.

The men — young and old — are just greedy for money whilst at the same time they are not willing to lift a finger, except in a rude gesture. They are only out to help themselves where there is money involved. They say one thing to your face — much like a dodgy used car dealer (Whoops! That's another term two millennia away!) Like I was saying, they will say one thing to your face with a big smile, but they lie through their teeth!

And the women move from house to house, like busy bees flying from one flower to another, as they gossip and spread the latest rumours. It would appear that no-one has ever taught any of these women the graces of hospitality or how to nurture the younger mothers. And, oh man, do they love their wine!

The scenario on this island gets worse, Paul. **SERIOUSLY!**

Now let me describe the young people — especially the young men. As you know me well, you would assume that I would gravitate to this generation — and yes, I do. And yet, this is where I struggle the most. These guys are my peer group, and I so much want to fit in. Yes, I am a Greek and I love to have a good time and hang out; but the more time I spend with these guys, the harder it is for me. I am torn! My flesh wants to belong and yet my heart is repulsed. Where do I fit in? How do I fit in? Can I — should I fit in? Again my head is spinning from the amount of work that you have left for me to do here!

Let me tell you about the Judaizers — and you know them only too well already. These religious dudes are not making it easy for anyone on this island who has chosen to be a follower of Jesus. Somehow they infiltrate the house churches, spruiking their rigid belief system of ritualistic circumcision. Actually, I'm wondering if you could 'CC' me a copy of the letter issued from the Jerusalem Council on this matter? Doh! Another 21st term ... sorry. Is it possible to get a hand written copy of it anyway?

You have always demonstrated what it means to speak the truth in love, Paul. "Full of grace" I recall. I'm wondering if these people would recognize the truth — even if it hit them like a tonne of bricks from the sky, or if it blew up in their faces like a giant firecracker! (Yeah, I know that gunpowder hasn't reached us yet via the Silk Road — as it's still a thousand years away!)

This society relies so much on the hard work of servants and slaves. I certainly do not envy their living conditions or renumerations. As I have tried to move amongst this hardworking cohort, I have observed that they murmur and complain all the time — speaking ill of their masters and bosses. Not only have I witnessed their disloyalty, I have also observed the efforts they go to, to cover up their pilfering from their bosses.

How can I possibly begin to combat the deception, lusts and passions of this community, when it seems like there is little or no self-control? I am struggling to see any hope for this place! And I fear — yes I fear! — I have very little to offer. The need here is just so enormous, and the people — yes I know God loves them and I'm trying to as well — but the people seem to be so ensnared in their ungodly behaviours, attitudes and mindset, including those whom you led to faith.

I know! I know! I can almost hear you from here shouting out loud, "Really Titus! Here he goes again, catastrophizing every little thing!

Come on son — **get a grip!"**

But please believe me Paul, when I say that I am just trying to be as honest as I can be. It's ok for you ... you are blessed with the gift of bold preaching, sound doctrinal teaching and the ability to argue persuasively. I've seen people come under your preaching with such conviction, and through your teaching of the Word, they are wonderfully

transformed by the Father's love for all humanity.
But ... I'm not you Paul!

I've seen you at work close up, and I've heard
you preach and teach on numerous occasions. Your
messages are so full of authority, power,
encouragement and grace. I know this well, as I have
had the extraordinary privilege of scribing a couple of
your letters. Knowing how you have a strong
commitment to living a life of godliness and humility.
You not only teach it and write about it — in fact,
you live it out daily! Your speech and your actions tell
the story of how your life was turned inside out and
upside down in a complete 180° direction. Ever since
I've known you — I have witnessed firsthand just
how your life, your attitudes and your deeds work
together through the power of the Holy Spirit —

modelling what it means to 'shout the mystery of godliness.'[3]

From experience, I know that you can be a very hard teacher Paul, and I do believe that when you deputed me to stay here on Crete, that you could already see the bigger picture of what was to come.

As you know me only too well, when I became a Christian, I quickly earned the reputation of 'that self-righteous Greek kid', who sees all the failures, flaws and fickle behaviours of my peers. On the other hand, you know that I have great respect for my elders, and for women. You also know that I am passionate about godly conduct — even though I don't get it right all the time, myself.

What I see everywhere I go, is that the daily lives of these new believers in Jesus are telling a story

— and that story is about an inherent resistance to transforming change.

So when you do reply Paul, I am actually anticipating some straight talking from you, delivering me some very direct instructions.

As I have already stated: I feel so much out of my depth here Paul. You are the one who preached and led these people to Christ. It's you they respect and look up to. I do not know even where to start, I also doubt that I would have any credibility, let alone any authority — especially because of my youthful looks. And I certainly do not feel courageous or strong amongst these Cretans who are 'short on virtue and long on vice'. [4] This is why I desperately need your advice and counsel, if I am to have any chance of

21

fashioning a healthy church community of loving disciples here on this island.

Being surrounded by everything I have described, only seems to bring back too many bad memories of my previous life Paul. Add to that, the longer I am here, I am beginning to feel as if I don't even know what to believe myself anymore. Maybe, it's that their lifestyle is drawing me back too far. If I am finding it hard to say 'no' to such things, how can I possibly have any chance of encouraging them towards saying 'yes' to godly behaviour?

And how can I possibly offer them any hope for their future? Where is their hope to be found? How can I begin to infiltrate their distorted belief system that doesn't even allow for an eternal hope?

These people — just like the Greeks — love a good debate. They will debate about anything, just for the sake of having a good argument! Their favourite topics seem to be centred around family trees and pedigrees — like who's related to whom and the prestige that accompanies any plausible links to royalty or fame.

Would you believe that there are even some men suggesting that because of my youthful physique that I could possibly be related to Alexander the Great! Can you believe that? I guess I will have to wait another 2000 years before I can take a DNA test to confirm that extraordinary genealogical possibility.

There are some men however, who vow and declare that they are related to Alexander, either directly or by intermarriage. Of course others hotly refute their claims.

On the other hand, some men even claim family links to Alexander's tutor, Aristotle. But even more incredible as it may sound, some of them as a matter of fact, go as far as claiming a direct ancestral connection to the Greek gods of Zeus, Leto, Artemis or Apollo.

Besides these genealogical debates, there are the Judaizers who want to argue over Jewish laws, and they get much pleasure through their constant refuting the gospel of grace.

I need to draw this letter to a close. But let me say this: it almost seems that they do not share any common purpose for good. They are so focussed on their own wants — short term and long term.

Please Paul, I need some answers here! What can I do in these situations? Is there any chance that you can provide some back up support for me . . . please?

Like I wrote earlier — I feel so alone and vulnerable. And I miss you terribly.

And before I sign off: Zenas and Apollos are keen to get on the move again. They've told me that they are just waiting for you to give the word.

Your son in the faith

Titus

End of SECTION ONE

INTERLUDE

Now that you have read Titus's epistle to Paul, it's time to read the paraphrased translation of Paul's epistle to Titus (The Voice™ translation).

By doing this relatively straight away, hopefully you will gain a deeper appreciation of Paul's encouragement, insights and instructions to his young protégé. You will also begin to note the subtle nuances between the two epistles. And in doing so, you will almost be able to hear Titus's deep sighs of relief, as well as him gritting his teeth as he summons all his physical, mental and spiritual strength urged on by his father in the faith. To press on ... to not stand for any nonsense ... to make godly decisions ... to rely on the Holy Spirit and hope in Christ Jesus ... and to hold true to godliness and sound doctrine.

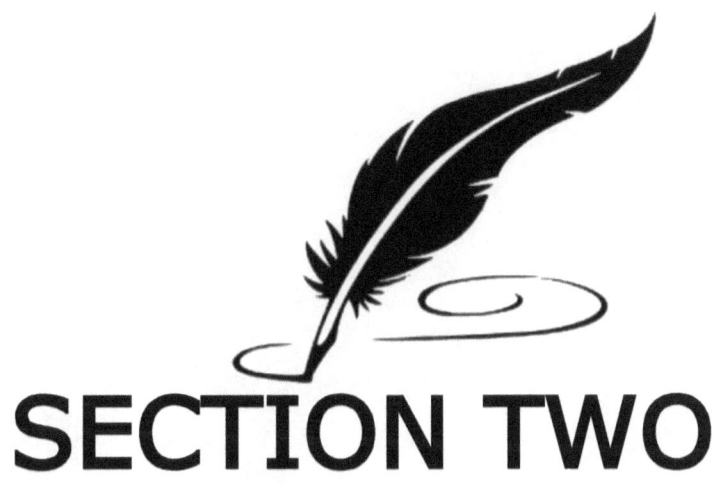

SECTION TWO

PAUL WRITES
TO TITUS

1 Paul, servant of God and emissary of Jesus, the Anointed One, on behalf of the faith that is accepted by God's chosen people and the knowledge of the undeniable truth that leads to godliness.

2 We rest in this hope we've been given—the hope that we will live forever with our God—the hope that He proclaimed ages and ages ago (even before time began). And our God is no liar; He is not even capable of uttering lies. 3 So we can be sure that it is in His exact right time that He released His word into the world—through the preaching that God our Savior has commanded into my care.

4 To you, Titus, my dear son birthed through our shared faith: may grace and peace rest upon you from God the Father and Jesus the Anointed, our Savior.

5 I left you on Crete so you could sort out the chaos and the unfinished business and appoint elders over communities in each and every city according to my earlier orders. 6 Here's what you should look for in an elder: he should be above suspicion; if he is married, he should be the husband of

one wife, raise children who believe, and be a person who can't be accused of rough and raucous living. 7 It is necessary that any overseer you appoint be blameless, as he is entrusted with God's mission. Look for someone who isn't pompous or quick to anger, who is not a drunkard, violent, or chasing after seedy gain or worldly fame. 8 Find a person who lovingly opens his home to others; who honors goodness; who is thoughtful, fair, devout, self-controlled; and 9 who clings to the faithful word that was taught because he must be able, not only to encourage people with sound teaching, but also to challenge those who are against it.

10 You see antagonists everywhere; they are rebellious, loose-lipped, and deceitful (especially those who are from the circumcised lot). 11 Their talk must be quashed—their mouths sealed up because impure teaching is flying out of their lips and overturning entire families for the sake of their own squalid gain. 12 I'll tell you, even their own prophet was heard saying, "Chronic liars, foul beasts, and lazy gluttons—that's who you'll meet in Crete." 13 And he's right! This is why we have to scold them, sometimes severely, so

they will be sound in the faith ¹⁴ and be able to ignore Jewish myths as well as any commandments given by those who turn away from the truth.

¹⁵ Listen: to those who are pure, all things are pure. But to those who are tainted, stained, and unbelieving, nothing is pure because their minds and their consciences are polluted. ¹⁶ They claim, "I know God," but their actions are a slap to His face. They are wretched, disobedient, and useless to any worthwhile cause.

2 As to you, Titus: talk to them; give them a good, healthy diet of solid teaching so they will know the right way to live.

² Here's what I want you to teach the older men: enjoy everything in moderation, respect yourselves and others, be sensible, and dedicate yourselves to living an unbroken faith demonstrated by your love and perseverance.

³ And here's what I want you to teach the older women: Be respectful. Steer clear of gossip or drinking too much so that you can teach what is good ⁴ to young women. Be a positive

example, showing them what it is to love their husbands and children, and teaching them to [5] control themselves in every way and to be pure. Train them to manage the household, to be kind, and to be submissive to their husbands, all of which honor the word of God.

[6] Encourage the young men in the same way: in every situation, they should learn to control themselves.

[7-8] Titus, you have to set a good example for everyone. Go out of your way to do what is right, speak the truth with the weight and authority that come from an honest and pure life. No one can argue with that. Then your enemies will cower in shame because they have nothing bad to say against us.

[9] Advise all the servants: Work hard for your masters, and be loyal to them. Strive to please. Don't be rude or sarcastic. [10] Don't steal or embezzle your masters' property. Show them you are trustworthy, and all the credit will go to the teaching of God our Savior.

[11] We have cause to celebrate because the grace of God has appeared, offering the gift of salvation to all people. [12] Grace arrives with its own instruction:

run away from anything that leads us away from God; abandon the lusts and passions of this world; live life now in this age with awareness and self-control, doing the right thing and keeping yourselves holy. 13 Watch for His return; expect the blessed hope we all will share when our great God and Savior, Jesus the Anointed, appears again. 14 He gave His body for our sakes and will not only break us free from the chains of wickedness, but He will also prepare a community uncorrupted by the world that He would call His own — people who are passionate about doing the right thing.

15 So, Titus, tell them all these things. Encourage and teach them with all authority—and rebuke them with the same. You are a man called to serve, so don't let anyone belittle you.

3 And remind them of this: respect the rulers and the courts. Obey them. Be ready to do what is good and honorable. 2 Don't tear down another person with your words. Instead, keep the peace, and be considerate. Be truly humble toward everyone 3 because there was a time when we, too, were foolish, rebellious, and deceived—we were slaves to

sensual cravings and pleasures; and we spent our lives being spiteful, envious, hated by many, and hating one another. ⁴But then something happened: God our Savior and His overpowering love and kindness for humankind entered our world; ⁵He came to save us. It's not that we earned it by doing good works or righteous deeds; He came because He is merciful. He brought us out of our old ways of living to a new beginning through the washing of regeneration; and He made us completely new through the Holy Spirit, ⁶who was poured out in abundance through Jesus the Anointed, our Savior. ⁷All of this happened so that through His grace we would be accepted into God's covenant family and appointed to be His heirs, full of the hope that comes from knowing you have eternal life. ⁸This is a faithful statement of what we believe.

Concerning this, I want you to put it out there boldly so that those who believe in God will be constant in doing the right things, which will benefit all of us. ⁹Listen, don't get trapped in brainless debates; avoid competition over family trees or pedigrees; stay away from fights and disagreements over the law.

They are a waste of your time. [10] If a person is causing divisions in the community, warn him once; and if necessary, warn him twice. After that, avoid him completely [11] because by then you are sure that you are dealing with a corrupt, sinful person. He is determined to condemn himself.

[12] I am sending either Artemas or Tychicus to you. When one of them arrives, try your best to make your way to me at Nicopolis (I plan to spend the winter there). [13] Do what you can to get Zenas (the lawyer) and Apollos on their way; make sure they have everything they need. [14] Our people must learn to get involved when a need arises, particularly when the need is urgent. Teach them to do what is good so they won't become unproductive members of the community.

[15] Everyone with me sends his greetings. Greet all our friends in the faith. May grace be with all of you. [Amen.] [5]

End of SECTION TWO

INTERLUDE

This last section — SECTION THREE — is quite the reverse of the process in the previous two SECTIONS. Let me explain.

Before reading into this next section, I recommend you take a break in time — a delay of perhaps a day or two. By doing so, you will allow the impact of the first sections to settle into your heart and mind.

When you are ready to move on, it is recommended that you re-read Paul's letter to Titus once again. On the basis this time that Titus is unaware of what Paul's letter may contain. Imagine Titus reading this letter for the first time after waiting for Paul's reply.

Use your imagination to determine the timespan from when Paul received Titus's letter till now.

How long was it?

Days? *Unlikely!*

Weeks? *Maybe.*

Months? *More than likely.*

Whatever the timespan, consider the relief in Titus's heart and mind when Paul's letter eventually arrived.

But hold the phone ... yet again?!

Now, let me throw you a curved ball here (actually, two curved balls).

First curved ball: Suppose ... just for a moment ... that the day after sending off his epistle to Paul by courier, Titus actually receives Paul's letter!

Wow! How did Paul know?

What prompted Paul to write to Titus ... as there is no possible way that he would have already received Titus's letter?

Second curved ball: now suppose if you will, that Titus did not even write to his mentor at all in the first place, before receiving Paul's letter. If we follow this train of thought it will mean that we will need to disregard all of SECTION ONE.

OK ... are you with me?

Now, just like any good choose-your-own-adventure story, you get to choose how you will read this next section. You can approach it either on the basis of the first notion ... or from the perspective of the second. Whichever way you choose, I submit to you this section as either a secondary-follow-up letter from Titus ... or an alternative single epistle from Titus to Paul in response to Paul's letter.

SECTION THREE

TITUS WRITES
TO PAUL

AFTER

HE RECEIVES

PAUL'S LETTER

Hey Paul

Thanks for your letter.

Where do I start?

Firstly, I have to acknowledge that you are indeed God's man for this generation of Gentile believers! Your awareness of the needs of God's people, no matter where they are from — who they are — or what their needs are, is such an incredible gift you have been given.

Thank you too for reminding me of the hope we've been given proclaimed long before time started ticking (hmm ... me thinks that *time is ticking* is a term yet to be coined for another 1500 years or so). To put it another way ... hope is eternal.

You have no idea (or maybe you do?) just how reassuring your reminder that God

is not a liar, nor is He even capable of telling
lies. It is just not in His nature. Especially as
I am surrounded by so much deception on
this island — the need for truth-telling is
at a crisis point here; and to be reminded
that our God is a truth-telling God, is like a
jab with an EpiPen of adrenalin to me
(Whoops! There's another term and
invention still two millennia away!).

Paul, I have been ranting and raving
for so long now about not knowing what to
do here. And I would not be surprised at all
if you already knew about that.

I am so stoked that you are my father
in the faith we now share, and with my
whole heart I gladly receive your blessing of
grace and peace. Even as I was unrolling
your scrolled letter to me, the Holy Spirit
filled my heart with such joy — reassuring

me that every frustrated concern that I have expressed either outwardly or sighed inwardly, the Lord already has it covered. God's timing hey?! So thank you for being obedient to the Spirit's prompting.

I have read and re-read your letter a dozen times now, and I really appreciate the way in which you have detailed my job description. To be honest Paul, in saying that I was really starting to wonder what in the heck I was meant to be doing here — in what appears to be an almost God-forsaken place. I am only now beginning to grasp through the chaos, why the 'unfinished business' — as you described it — needs attending to.

You have written about appointing elders and overseers who are blameless! Seeking out those men who are above suspicion is going to be a real challenge; especially as the outspoken men who crave being in the limelight, definitely seem to stifle the few quieter men who do show some degree of integrity.

Paul, the way in which you describe an overseer as blameless, helps me see why he is to be entrusted with God's mission of leading the Church. You tend to use the words overseer and elder in a way like they were on the interchange bench (although nobody has thought of the big-league game interchange bench concept as yet!)

As I was saying — before I interrupted myself — realising that an elder does not necessarily have to be a high-flyer (oh boy ... these 20th century terms keep popping out almost prophetically!) — someone who grabs for power, or money or fame; but one who is considerate, hospitable, has Godly values, decent, devout and self-controlled. I get that ... really, I do!

As I am now understanding this Paul, an elder should not be swayed by either popularity, false teaching or money. On the contrary, they need to be willing to hold onto the word of truth — the gospel message you taught them — as well as having the desire and ability to encourage others in replicating such teaching.

I realise that such men and women need to be strong in character — not only do they need to be strong enough to refrain from binge drinking, but they also need to be strong enough to stand up against those who loosely claim to have faith, and especially against those who are peddling such false teaching.

After reading and re-reading your letter many times, the Holy Spirit has already begun revealing to me a few names of people I can approach and appoint as elders. One idea that has just occurred to me is the possibility of co-opting the service of some of the men for a community service project — such as a Men's Shed to make toys for disadvantaged kids, or to develop a community garden. These men might be a mixture of some high flyers as well as the quiet achievers who stay under the radar (oh … here we go with another term still centuries away!) The challenge will be in promoting the idea as a volunteer project for the benefit of the community rather than a money-spinning venture.

The twisting ache in my gut has eased considerably and my head is a lot clearer, now. The more I have meditated on what you have written, as being the word of the Lord; confusion and despair have distanced themselves from me.

Having said that, and the fact that you have encouraged me so much, you have also challenged me in the midst of my cloudy thoughts and despondency. Yes, you have called me to task — to step up to the plate (to use another phrase still 1800 years from now) — to take action because something needs to be done, even though it will be difficult. The time is right for me to take my stance — using my God-given talents and abilities — to throw down the gauntlet (to use a metaphor from the middle ages) — in taking on the antagonists and the loud mouths.

I love the way you have quoted from one of their own prophetic poets, depicting the behavioural mindset on this island of Crete:

"Chronic liars,

foul beasts

and lazy gluttons"

I think I'm going to use that line! Just like holding a mirror up in their faces ... with grace and respect ... of course!

Even now, as I write, I can sense the Holy Spirit's empowerment and wisdom welling up inside me — equipping me — preparing me to tackle those Judaizers, who spruik about claiming to 'know God'. And just as you rightly point out ... their claims are insulting to the Lord when their actions and motives reveal otherwise.

As I consider the direct challenge you have given me to be strong and gentle in talking to people — I realise just how much I have been doubting myself. Fearing that I had little to offer, with little credibility or authority. I guess, now as I reflect on the past few months, in moving about through these small communities, all the while God has been preparing me for this next phase of the work.

Your letter has given me a good kick in the pants Paul! What I have been fearing has been given a good shake up into a realisation that I need to be proactive — rather than reactive. The best way I can describe this wake-up call is, as if a giant hand has slapped my face shouting:

"Wake up Titus!

I've got your back!

You can do this this!

I know where you live!

I know you!

I believe in you!"

God has spoken directly to me through your words!

Ironically though, at the same time, I have also had the sensation of being tenderly cuddled like a huge embracing huggle of love and acceptance and reassurance.

So, in practical terms, I have begun creating a plan of action. I am going to invite a couple of women to help me organise a series of events — starting with Crete's Biggest Morning Tea. The co-opted women's role will be to spread the news — and believe me they are good at that! The idea is to bring a plate of food and dress up for the occasion. I plan to make this an alcohol-free event, although it will not be promoted as such for we will have an ample supply of the refreshing *Tsai tou vounou* or Mountain Tea. [6]

Once the women are gathered together, sipping their tea and filling their faces, I will put on my best welcoming voice — tell a few funny stories segueing into the downfalls of gossiping and over-indulging in wine. I pray that I may have the boldness and grace to be able to pull this off.

My ideas to draw them in, are firstly to set up a game of Chinese Whispers (although I'm not sure why it is called that … except that the more we talk, the less we listen, and so too the less decipherable our conversations become).

For the second morning tea, I will invite a few of the women up to do some role-playing scenarios. Highlighting the importance of respectfully showing love to their husbands and children. I'm sure this will provide quite a few belly laughs, but I am also confident that these scenarios will play out in such a way that there will be quite a bit of squirming in their seats ... resulting in conviction towards changes in domestic relationships and behaviour.

For the third and final morning tea event, as an incentive / bonus for those who by now may be of the opinion that I am just a self-righteous teetotaler; I will advertise the function as a Ca'lida [7] and Passum [8] wine tasting.

For this final workshop opportunity, I am planning to introduce some strategy games designed for nurturing self-control in a variety of circumstances. The first part of the program will be prior to the Ca'lida and Passum testing. The second part will be the taste testing, after which we conclude with a couple more strategy games. My intention is to help them experience the importance of exercising self-control, both with and without the influence of wine and to understand the difference.

Throughout the 3-week program, I will intentionally be seeking out a few women, who display restraint from gossip and self-indulgence, whilst showing enthusiasm, encouragement, hospitality and domestic initiative. Hmmm ... I hope that's not asking too much, is it?!

Paul, having received and pondered your direct talking in your letter, I can now appreciate the fact that I am equipped when it comes to teaching on sound doctrine. After all ... look at who my mentor is?! In fact your letter will become my 'exhibit A' and I myself this time will be 'exhibit B'! Not like in Jerusalem where I was your 'exhibit A'!

I'm very glad — and relieved — that we both agree on the two essential issues to be addressed here on Crete: solid teaching of sound doctrine, and the mastery of self-control. Especially regarding the younger men, in order to bring about lasting generational change within the church community. I know that I am going to have to step into the ring - so to speak - and clearly demonstrate that in every situation it is possible to be in charge of oneself and not get out of control.

Again, this is one of those situations that I do wish I lived in another time zone! I mean can you just envisage taking a bunch of these young guys out into a Paintball Field! Hmmm … now that's certainly got my creative juices flowing.

As I think about it, maybe we could use some animal gizzard skins and fill them with some sort of colouring dye powder. There's no shortage of gizzard skins here. And there's plenty of dyes available in the markets as well — plant-based dyes like crocus sativus (ochres), madder, woad, weld (yellow), walnut hulls, oak gall (brown and black), orchil lichen (pink/purple), alchanet (red), and saffron crocus (yellow). And as well there's a ready supply of animal-based dyes like kermes beetles (red/cochineal) and seashell creatures such as spiny (purple) dye-murex, and the red-mouthed rock shell (purple). [9]

And the more I think about it, I'm already beginning to feel tickled pink — or should I say ... red and purple and yellow?! I am so excited! This activity will provide such a great release of energy in contrast to tea parties!

These young guys would love to be involved in this project from go to whoa for sure! Some of the guys could be assigned the task of gathering the necessary materials, others to manufacture the gizzard balls, and others to search out the best corner of the forest for the event. I'm sure that word will get around quickly in this community. Now, let me think ... what shall we call this event? 'Gizzard Ball Games?' 'Hot Shots?' 'Dye Hard Games?' I think I'll let them choose. Bring it on!!

Activities such as this will provide situational awareness and opportunities for me to share my own testimony. I can tell my story of how Jesus has rescued me from going down the wrong path and how his Spirit sustains me 'to do what is right', to speak the truth based on the strength and authority that comes from living an honest life of purity and integrity.

You mentioned the servants, Paul. Not having been a servant or having had one myself, I realise that I must somehow earn their trust. I'm thinking that I must factor-in some time to volunteer to work alongside them. Plus, I realise that I will need to gain approval from their masters before taking any other actions. I'm thinking if I can begin helping them in their servant tasks, I will have a better chance of earning their respect — not so much as an 'undercover boss' — but as one who can demonstrate good work ethics of respect and honesty. In doing any of this, my intention is to give all the credit to the Lord.

Thank you Paul for clarifying the virtually ethereal concept of grace. As you have simply expressed, it is God's 'gift of salvation to all people.' Then you expand on that by saying when grace arrives it brings with it the ability [to] 'run away from anything that leads us away from God; [to] abandon the lusts and passions of this world; [to] live life now in this age *with awareness* and self-control, doing the right thing [because it is the right thing to do] and keeping [ourselves] holy.' Wow! What incredible benefits grace offers! This has given me a whole new perspective on the 'expected blessed hope' ... like you say ... as we watch for Jesus' return.

The image you have painted with the expression "free from the chains of wickedness", no doubt will strike a note of additional hope for the servants. It will undoubtedly lift their spirits — particularly those who have been enslaved to merciless masters.

Paul, you seemed to have nailed it when you addressed the issue of respect. I can visualize the vertical and horizontal dimensions of respect, and how it works out in practical ways:

Vertically: towards those in authority — bosses, rulers and the legal system.

Horizontally: towards others in our peer groups and beyond.

Respect towards others has a circular motion on a 360° axis.

So, what goes around comes around!

The flipside of this cyclical concept as I see it, is that disrespect and dishonour going hand-in-hand have permeated every sector of this community — both secular and Christian.

I absolutely l-o-v-e your statement Paul, of 'what we believe'! It is so powerfully expressed!

He [Jesus] came to save us ...

He came because He is merciful ...

He brought us out ...

He made us completely new ...

All of this happened ... so that we would be accepted ... full of hope ...

[Having] eternal life!

Wow!

And doing the right thing consistently — not as goodie two shoes but as believers in the Living God, as you rightly point out — will benefit everyone. In my own way of explaining it ...

doing the right thing because it is the right thing to do ...

... results from the grace and hope we have in Jesus.

And by the way, let me tell you, I have already discovered just how easily one can be sucked into their senseless debates masqueraded as conversations about fake news or current affairs. These people — just like the Greeks — love a good debate, and they will debate about anything and everything, just for the sake of having a good argument!

Now, I'm fairly sure that this type of discussion is not just a 21st century phenomenon — these people also squabble about weather, politics, finances, sport and the legal system. So, I guess even in 2023 someone will realise that there is nothing new under the sun!

Part of my steep learning curve has involved being so easily drawn into the futility of ancestral exploration, where one person claims to be related to one of the Greek gods, and another claiming to be a distant offspring of Alexander the Great, through intermarriage! Someone even suggested that I could be related to Alexander because of my youthful looks! And yes, pride crept in for just a brief moment ... and I was hoodwinked!

I must admit that I had been wondering what your advice might be regarding dealing with the trouble maker(s) causing divisions within the Church community. Having read your counsel, I will trust the Holy Spirit to give me the words — pluck up the courage — and warn them once. And if necessary, graciously issue another warning. Then, if there is no change in their behaviour, whilst still being respectful — trying to avoid them will be a challenge!

I get what you are saying Paul — really I do get it! I'm not to ignore division of any sort in any way. I realise that I will need to exercise the authority I have in the Lord, to deal with these matters, in order for this

Church community to grow strong and to be in unity.

Now before I sign off: Zenas and Apollos are keen to get on the move again. They've asked me to tell you, that they are just waiting for you to give the word.

Your son in the faith

Titus

End of SECTION THREE

FINAL WORD

Titus may have or may not have written to his mentor Paul — more than likely not. However, this book has been intentionally written to highlight the issues which confronted this young man on the island of Crete.

Having considered both the speculative and the reflective writings of these epistles, and the values of a 'good' lifestyle; it comes as no surprise as to how alluring and yet how shunned these values are in today's world. "So what's new?" we may well ask.

The paradox is that in many ways, the post-Christian society we live in, is somehow still curiously attracted to these values.

After all, more than ever, our society wants (*no ... demands actually*) to see integrity in leadership — whether in sport, politics, business or the church. And besides, who doesn't want older men and women to be temperate and admirable, worthy of respect and exhibiting wisdom and love?

Likewise, who could not be attracted to the idea of a devoted, pure young woman unpolluted by the world's enticements, who has been taught to love and respect her husband and children — mentored by an older, wiser woman?

And what boss or employer would not want their workers to be respectful, hard-working and trustworthy?

Oh, and how today's society is crying out for — demanding — principled, self-controlled, decent young men! Our daily news reports are full of the exact opposite! They appear so out of control.

All the while, our society longs for such a set of values like this and yet, conversely, when confronted with them, society on the whole, refuses to live this way. Another paradox here, is that when Christians try to live out these values, they are ridiculed.

In our current culture of wokeism — there are those who are chaffing at the bit to wipe us off, at our slightest slip up. We find ourselves in conflict with our workmates when we choose to act honestly, especially when we see them abusing the system.

Truth telling is talked about on a variety of fronts these days, and yet telling the truth — even amongst Christians — seems to have lost its credence and meaning in godly living.

We are belittled by our peers when we choose decency over self-indulgence, and honour over shame and scandal. We are pressured on all sides to go with the flow in people-pleasing and self-pleasing; to embrace the same avaricious, self-centred lifestyle as our neighbours; and to sacrifice family life to the gods of achievements, money or momentary popularity and fame.

The standards of all this irrefutable conduct outlined by Paul, which Titus has speculatively questioned in this book, have highlighted for us an entirely radical alternative lifestyle. A lifestyle that is motivated by God's grace through Christ, which Paul describes as 'pleasing to God.' Or as one theologian said: "[we are to] model the gospel by giving it a human face, a living pattern that others can relate to and follow". [10]

May we ... may you and I ... through the power of the Holy Spirit, endeavour to live our lives in such a way that pleases God the Father and glorifies Jesus, the Son.

APPENDIX

DISCUSSION
QUESTIONS

📖 What insights (if any) have you gained from reading this book?

📖 If you were Titus, are there any other questions you think you might have asked Paul? Is there anything you would have like Paul to have explained further?

📖 How has this book helped you better understand the church situation on Crete? What is the stand-out issue for you?

📖 Re-read 'The Voice translation' of Paul's epistle to Titus, then read it in a couple of other translations. What do you notice? What are the similarities or stand-out differences?

📖 Which of Titus's epistles gives you the best insight into his character? Do you think that both letters describe the same personality traits? How are they different?

📖 Which of Titus's epistles do you prefer? Why?

📖 If you were Titus, would you preferred to have received Paul's letter before or after you had written your letter?

📖 What is the most stand-out truth or insight you can walk away with from this book?

📖 Can you see any similarities between the church on Crete, and the current church situation worldwide, nationally, denominationally, or local? What things do we have in common?

📖 Paul's epistle to Titus is not about developing a 'good' lifestyle but rather about developing a 'godly' lifestyle. How is this achievable in the 21st century?

Further recommended study notes on Titus

- The Path to Godliness by Phillip D Jensen & Tony Payne, Matthias Media, 1992

ENDNOTES

&

BIBLIOGRAPHY

1. NIV Bible
2. NIV Bible
3. The VOICE™ Commentary—Titus
4. The VOICE™ Commentary—Titus
5. The Voice™. Copyright © 2012 by Ecclesia Bible Society.
6. Mountain tea is a naturally caffeine-free herbal tea made from a single variety of the sideritis plant. Also known as "Shepherd's Tea" or "Greek Mountain Tea," it is referred to in Greece as *Tsai tou vounou*, translating directly to "Tea of the mountain." It is brewed using the dried flowers, leaves, and stems of the sideritis plant, found in the Mediterranean mountain regions of Greece.
   https://www.allrecipes.com/article/what-is-mountain-tea-sideritis/

7. A Dictionary of Greek and Roman Antiquities, John Murray, London, 1875.
8. A Dictionary of Greek and Roman Antiquities, John Murray, London, 1875
9. https://en.wikipedia.org/
10. Douglas Milne (source unknown)
11. https://dictionary.cambridge.org/

Gary Lewis is a retired Primary School Chaplain and more recently a mentor to School Chaplains. His background is Primary School education, Children's Ministry, and Church Pastor — covering more than 50 years of ministry. His extensive lay ministry has also included Worship Leading, Preaching, Prayer Ministry Coordinator and Church eldership over many years.

As well as books on prayer, he has also authored several children's books — picture story books and novels — all of which are based on true stories from his chaplaincy work with primary-aged students. He has also been sharing stories through being a blogger for more than fifteen years https://life-markers.blogspot.com/

Gary's books are available at:

https://www.garylewisbooks.com/

OTHER BOOKS BY GARY LEWIS

- ➢ VERTICALLY CHALLENGED: *the ups and downs of praying* (2022)

- ➢ PRAYER BUBBLES: *turning thoughts into prayers for hesitants* (2023)

- ➢ LITTLE BOY ALL LOCKED UP (2023)

- ➢ STOLEN TRUTH and the DARK HOODED THIEF (2023)

- ➢ NOT FOR LITTLE BOYS (2021)

- ➢ STOLEN TRUTH and the FACE in the SHATTERED MIRROR (2023)

- ➢ AGING BRAINS...ANCIENT GAMES (2023)

- ➢ JESSICA finds her true VALUE (2017)

- ➢ JACKSON UNCOVERS HIDDEN TREASURE (2017)

- ➢ OLIVIA'S jar of PICKLED INSPIRATION (2021)

www.ingramcontent.com/pod-product-compliance
Lightning Source LLC
Chambersburg PA
CBHW030416120726
47904CB00007B/2304